Bad Luck Boswell

Written & illustrated by
Diane Dawson Hearn

Simon & Schuster Books for Young Readers

SIMON & SCHUSTER BOOKS FOR YOUNG READERS
An imprint of Simon & Schuster Children's Publishing Division
1230 Avenue of the Americas, New York, New York 10020

Copyright © 1995 by Diane Dawson Hearn

All rights reserved including the right of reproduction in whole or in
part in any form.

SIMON & SCHUSTER BOOKS FOR YOUNG READERS is a trademark of Simon & Schuster.

Book design by Cathy Bobak
The text for this book is set in 14 point ITC Berkeley Oldstyle.
The illustrations were done in pen, ink, and acrylics.
Manufactured in the United States of America

First edition
10   9   8   7   6   5   4   3   2   1

Library of Congress Cataloging-in-Publication Data
Hearn, Diane Dawson.
Bad luck Boswell / Diane Dawson Hearn. — 1st ed.
p.   cm.
Summary: Boswell the cat brings bad luck to everyone he meets,
including a nasty witch with mean intentions.
ISBN 0-689-80303-6
[1. Cats—Fiction.   2. Luck—Fiction.   3. Witches—Fiction.]
I. Title.
PZ7.H3455Bad   1995
[E]—dc20   94-10850

Another one for Mom and Dad

From the beginning, Boswell had a hard life. All his brothers and sisters were taken into loving homes, but nobody wanted him. Because he was black, the superstitious villagers feared him. So although he was a remarkably friendly and kindhearted cat, he was left to wander the streets alone. And wherever he went, misfortune seemed to follow.

No sooner would Boswell come meowing for a little scratch behind the ears than *whack*, the cobbler would hammer his thumb instead of a shoe.

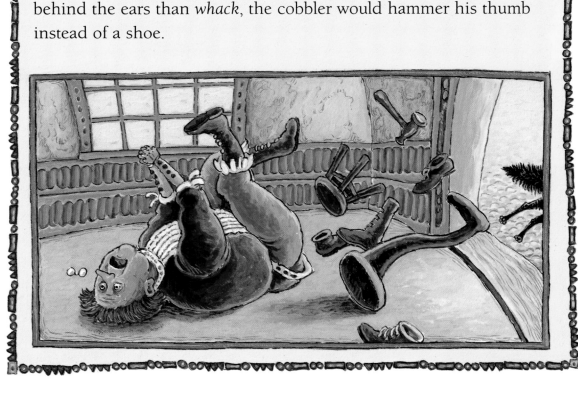

If Boswell rubbed himself against the milkmaid's legs, hoping for a little lap of cream, *whoops*, down she would go, spilling all her milk onto the road. And when Boswell merely crossed paths with the mayor, the old man was certain to catch cold the very next day.

Before long, the villagers were calling him Bad Luck Boswell. Whenever he passed by, people would hide themselves to avoid his bad luck. Boswell felt terrible; he never wanted to cause anyone harm. At last he decided sadly that the only solution was to leave town.

He found a place under the ruins of an old bridge, where he lived as best he could on minnows and field mice.

The villagers were not sorry to see him go. Once again, their lives were quiet and predictable, and they were content.

At times Boswell would creep to the edge of town just to watch as children played beside snug cottages. Then, sighing, he would return to his life of solitude.

Some months later, a witch moved into the old tower on the hill. The villagers were terrified. They could tell by the ugly pendant dangling from her scrawny neck that she belonged to the Coven of Darkness, which meant she was nasty through and through. When she flew into town, the people hid, trembling, behind locked doors.

"So you won't give a poor old woman a decent welcome, eh?" the witch shouted as she stood alone in the village square. "Won't even sell me a crock of beans for my supper, eh? Well, I'll teach you to be a mite more friendly to strangers. You'll be sorry. Very sorry."

With that she stormed out of town, mumbling threats. As she soared over the old ruined bridge, she spied Boswell sunning himself, half asleep.

"That black cat will give me the power I need to hex those wretched villagers," she thought. With a gleeful shriek she swooped down, grabbed the startled cat, and plunked him onto her broomstick. "You're coming home with me," said the witch. "I've always wanted a black cat."

Boswell's whiskers began to tingle. Had he heard correctly? This person actually wanted him? Crouching behind her on the broomstick, Boswell stared as the ground whooshed away. His tail twitched with excitement. He was going home!

Crack! Crash! Suddenly the broomstick plowed into a huge pine tree. Being a cat, Boswell leaped nimbly onto a branch. The witch wasn't as fortunate. In a cloud of pinecones and needles she landed with a hard thud. The broomstick was splintered beyond repair.

"Where did that tree come from?" the witch screamed, kicking what was left of the broomstick. "Now we'll have to walk."

Boswell hesitated. His bad luck had caused that accident, he knew, and was bound to cause others. He should run away at once. Yet… his tail wagged furiously in confusion. He wanted so much to go home with her, to sit on her lap beside a warm fire. He could almost taste the sweet cream she would give him.

"Come on, cat," the witch hollered as she stomped off.

Boswell jumped down from the branch and followed her into the woods.

The bad luck did bring more trouble again and again.

By the time the witch hobbled up the steep path leading to her tower, she was red eyed with fury. Boswell slunk along guiltily behind her, knowing he should leave. But home was so close now.

"What could be causing all these catastrophes?" grumbled the witch as she entered the tower. "Well, I'm bound to be safe in my own house."

She reached for a torch to light her way, but it was stuck in its holder. "Hmmph." The witch tugged with both hands on the torch.

Pop! Out came the torch. Caught off balance, the witch careened into an old suit of armor. *Clonk! Clang!* As the witch and the armor tumbled into a heap, the torch rolled to a stop beside a rope that held a heavy chandelier. In less than a minute, the rope burned through, and the walls shook as the chandelier fell, smashing the dining table and chairs.

"Water! Water!" yelled the witch, dashing outside to the well. While Boswell gaped helplessly, she frantically tossed pails of water at the flames until they were all doused.

The witch collapsed onto a chair. Glaring at the soggy remains of her dining hall, she shook her head. "Never saw such rotten luck in all my days."

Boswell sighed. Better to leave now, he thought, before causing any more disasters.

"Where do you think you're going?" the witch snarled when she noticed Boswell creeping away. "I'm fairly itching to cast a nasty spell on those stupid villagers, and I need your black-cat power to help me do it. Come on." With that she yanked Boswell up by the scruff of the neck and began to climb the tower stairs.

Black-cat power? Nasty spell? Boswell began to squirm and hiss as he realized what was going on. She had never planned to give him a nice home. She had merely wanted to use him for her evil purposes. He tried to escape, but before he could scratch his way to freedom, she had him locked up in the tower. There she began to brew her concoction, cackling and muttering all the while. Perched on a shelf above the cauldron, Boswell gazed into the bubbling mess. It looked and smelled a lot like the slimy, stagnant pond near his old bridge.

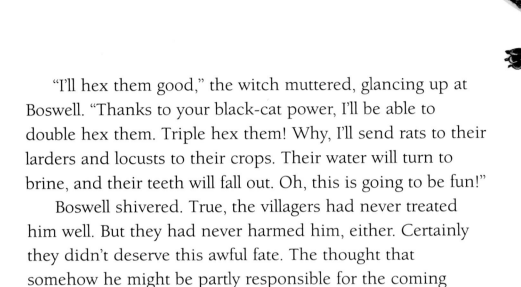

"I'll hex them good," the witch muttered, glancing up at Boswell. "Thanks to your black-cat power, I'll be able to double hex them. Triple hex them! Why, I'll send rats to their larders and locusts to their crops. Their water will turn to brine, and their teeth will fall out. Oh, this is going to be fun!"

Boswell shivered. True, the villagers had never treated him well. But they had never harmed him, either. Certainly they didn't deserve this awful fate. The thought that somehow he might be partly responsible for the coming calamity made the fur on his tail stick straight out.

Something had to be done. When the witch raised her arms and began to chant some evil-sounding words, Boswell could see that she was almost finished. Would his mere presence be enough to ruin the spell? Boswell never knew how his bad luck worked. This time he had to make sure that it did.

Suddenly the witch pointed at the cauldron. "And now for the final curse!" she screamed.

But before she could utter another word, with a fearful yowl Boswell flung himself into the cauldron.

The explosion was seen for miles around. In the village, buildings shook and windows cracked. Ashes rained down for hours. When the sky cleared, the villagers noticed that nothing was left of the tower on the hill. They never saw the witch again.

Three days later, Boswell wobbled into town, his fur singed and matted, his body gaunt from hunger. It was obvious to everyone that he had lost at least one of his nine lives in the explosion.

"Look what he's got!" exclaimed the milkmaid when Boswell dropped the pendant he had carried back from the tower. "That thing belonged to the witch."

"Why, it's Boswell put a whammy on the witch," said the cobbler. "Bad Luck Boswell saved our skins."

"He helped us even though we didn't want him around," the milkmaid added softly. "What a fine creature."

Everyone crowded around the black cat then, petting him and
offering him tasty tidbits. They were so grateful that they forgot to
be afraid of his bad luck. And for the first time in his whole life,
Boswell purred.

"I propose that we adopt Boswell as our official Town Cat," said
the mayor. "True, he may bring a bit of bad luck to some of us now
and again, but what's that compared with a witch?"

Everyone cheered their agreement.

So Boswell was given his own cozy room in Town Hall. The villagers took turns feeding him, and they fed him well. He had the run of the town. When he was not playing Chase the String with the village children, he could be seen sunning himself on the Town Hall steps, where everyone stopped to pet him. A happier cat would have been hard to find.

Strangely enough, although everyone expected it, Boswell never again brought the villagers misfortune. They decided that the life Boswell had lost in the explosion was his unlucky one. The town thrived again, as it had before the witch came along. And whenever outsiders asked the reason for this success, the villagers smiled. "See that cat?" they would say, pointing to Boswell. "Wherever he goes, he brings good luck."